HAPPY DREAMS, LITTLE BUNNY

LEAH HONG

Little, Brown and Company
New York Boston

For my little bunnies,
Mary and Thomas

Mommy, I can't sleep.

What's the matter, Little Bunny?

I keep wondering if I'll stay small forever. Will I ever be big?

I can see why your thoughts are keeping you up.
What if you turned some of these thoughts into dreams?

I could try....

It won't be hard, Little Bunny,
with your imagination.

Maybe Elephant can help!
In my dreams, Elephant will be real.

How perfect. What will you do together?

We'll have lots of adventures, all by ourselves.

First, we'll go to the beach and play. We'll pretend we're giants.

That sounds like fun. What will you do next?

I want to try flying.
If I'm small enough,
then I can ride a bumblebee.

Be sure to hold on tight!

I will! And when I get hungry, we can stop for a snack.

Healthy snacks to help you grow bigger?

So healthy that Elephant and I will grow our own wings! We'll fly into the sky together.

Where will you go?

We'll soar over the ocean until we find the tallest lighthouse, and we'll climb all the way to the top to make sure nothing crashes into it.

How brave you and Elephant will be!

We'll be so brave, we'll climb past the lighthouse and into space.

Will you be gone for long?

Long enough to go to the moon and back!

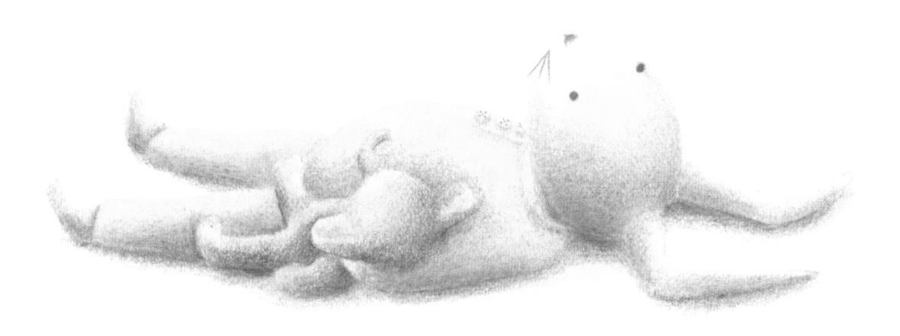

My goodness, that could take a while.

Well, we can come home anytime we want, because we can slide all the way back to Earth.

How wonderful. Where will I be when you return?

You'll be here, picking out books for us to read together…

NEW
BOOKSELLERS
USED
89
OPEN

…and I can climb inside the pages and go anywhere.

I'd love to do that for you, Little Bunny. It sounds like you're going to have a very busy night. Do you think you're ready to begin your adventures now? Can I bring you back to your bed?

Okay…but, Mommy?

Yes, Little Bunny?

I think Elephant's already asleep.

I think you're right.

Good night, Little Bunny. Happy dreams.

About This Book

The illustrations for this book were done in pastel, pencil crayon, and graphite. This book was edited by Andrea Spooner, art directed by Sasha Illingworth, and designed by Angelie Yap. The production was supervised by Bernadette Flinn, and the production editor was Marisa Finkelstein. The text was set in Bembo, and the display type was hand-lettered by Leah Hong.

 • Little, Brown and Company • Hachette Book Group • 1290 Avenue of the Americas, New York, NY 10104 • Visit us at LBYR.com • First Edition: February 2021 • Little, Brown and Company is a division of Hachette Book Group, Inc. • The Little, Brown name and logo are trademarks of Hachette Book Group, Inc. • The publisher is not responsible for websites (or their content) that are not owned by the publisher. • Library of Congress Cataloging-in-Publication Data • Names: Hong, Leah, author, illustrator. • Title: Happy dreams, Little Bunny / Leah Hong. • Description: New York : Little, Brown and Company, 2021. | Audience: Ages 4–8. | Summary: When Little Bunny is restless at bedtime, Mommy encourages him to imagine the adventures he will have in his dreams once he is asleep. • Identifiers: LCCN 2019031290 | ISBN 9780316536011 (hardcover) • Subjects: CYAC: Bedtime—Fiction. | Imagination—Fiction. | Adventure and adventurers—Fiction. | Mothers and sons—Fiction. | Rabbits—Fiction. • Classification: LCC PZ7.1.H65452 Hap 2021 | DDC [E]—dc23 • LC record available at https://lccn.loc.gov/2019031290 • ISBN: 978-0-316-53601-1 (hardcover) • PRINTED IN CHINA • APS • 10 9 8 7 6 5 4 3 2 1